Under the Skin

by

Catherine MacPhail

Illustrated by Tom Percival

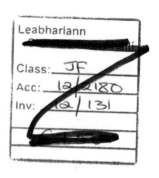

First published in 2007 in Great Britain by
Barrington Stoke Ltd
18 Walker St, Edinburgh, EH3 7LP

www.barringtonstoke.co.uk

This edition first published 2012

ISBN: 978-1-78112-083-5

Printed in China by Leo

Contents

Chapter 1
A Letter to My Cousin

My dear cousin Chat,

I am writing my letters in English because when you come to this country to live, you must speak good English. When I first came here I did not speak good English. I said all the wrong words. It was very embarrassing. I had a face that was red all the time.

I do not want you to make the same mistakes. My friend, Sam, will help you.

And you will come soon, Chat. Do not give up hope. One day you and your father will join my family in this wonderful country.

I will tell you of my house. I live on the top floor, the 15th floor of a beautiful tower block. It is a penthouse apartment and the tower block is right in the middle of the city. We have a balcony and a fantastic view. From our balcony we can see the river as it opens out into the sea. They call this city the dear green place, and when you come you will see why. There are trees and grass and parks all around us.

We have a bathroom and a kitchen in our house. The only thing I do not like is that I have to sleep in the same room as my little sisters. This is not good. Their bedroom is painted in pink. Yuk! I m a boy. Boys do not sleep in pink bedrooms. And my sisters fight all the time. They throw things at each other. Last night a flying hairbrush hot me on the head.

Since I have come to this country, I have learned that I do not like fighting. My friend Sam has made me see that fighting does not get you anywhere. It is better to try to be friends with people.

Sam lives on the 10th floor of this same tower block. He goes to the same school as I do. In fact, he is in the same class. This is the same school you will go to when you come here. Our teacher is Mrs Hart. She is a very good teacher, but she shouts a lot. I must go now. Or I will be late for class. And Mrs Hart shouts very loud if we are late. I will write again soon.

Your cousin, Omar

****

"Are you ready for school?" my father shouts.

I put the letter into the envelope, and it goes into my bag.

"I'm ready, Father," I tell him.

My father was a doctor back in my country. But the government said he was looking after the wrong people, and put him in prison. Here in this country, he can't work at all, until they decide if we can stay. That makes my father very sad. He likes to work. I pray every night that we won't be sent back. I'm afraid about getting sent back. If we stay, then my father'll be a doctor again, he says. And I know he will.

My father can do anything. He got us here to safety, didn't he?

I meet Mrs Brown as I wait for the lift. Mrs Brown lives next door to us. She does not smile. She never smiles. Her face is set like stone.

"Good morning," I say, as I always do.

She turns up her hearing aid. She's as deaf as a doorpost, Sam says. I don't understand why people here say this. You expect a doorpost to be deaf. It doesn't have ears, does it? English is a very funny language.

"Did you get your toilet fixed?" she snaps at me.

She must see I don't understand at once. She speaks slowly as if I'm very stupid.

"Your toilet was blocked. Have you had it fixed?"

Now, I understand. I nod. "Yes, Mrs Brown. Our toilet now works fine." I'm thinking how kind she is to ask. Perhaps she was ready to let us, our whole family, use her toilet.

I should know better by now.

Mrs Brown begins to speak to the invisible friend she always has by her side. The friend she always talks to but who no one can see. "What do you think of that! I've been waiting six months to get my sink unblocked, and they get their toilet fixed just like that!"

She snaps her fingers in front of my face.

I almost tell her that this isn't true. My mother's been moaning for a long time about the toilet. But Mrs Brown is still talking to her pretend friend. The invisible one.

"They got a fridge for nothing, didn't they?" she says to this friend.

I know she isn't talking to me but I answer her even so. "Yes," I tell her. "People have been very kind."

"Ha!" she says. "I had to buy my fridge. Always the same. I have to work for everything and you get it for nothing."

I worked out long ago that Mrs Brown is as daft as a brush. That's how they say it here. "Daft as a brush." I don't know why. Brushes aren't any more daft than any other tool around the house. Why don't they say daft as a dustbin? I don't understand. English is very difficult to learn.

All I wish now is that the lift would hurry up. Mrs Brown scares me.

At least today the lift's working. It arrives at our floor and the doors creak open. I step inside. Mrs Brown does not. She decides to go back to her own flat and moan to someone else about her sink that's blocked. I'm glad to see that she takes her invisible friend with her.

The lift goes on down. Then it stops at the tenth floor. Sam steps inside.

He pretends he doesn't see me. "What's that smell?" he says and he sniffs like a dog. Then he looks down his nose at me. "Oh, it's wee Omar." And he pushes me against the wall.

I do my best to go to school at a different time to Sam. He's always late. I'm always early. But today I was writing my letter to my cousin and so I'm late too.

I try to ignore him. But he won't let me. He pulls me round to face him. He calls me names. He shouts into my face. "Got nothing to say, eh?"

I hold my breath. I know what's going to happen next.

Chapter 2
Sam and Me

You think I'm going to say he hits me?

No. I hit him.

I land a punch right on his face. Sam yells, and he falls back onto the floor of the lift, holding on to his nose. There's a spurt of blood. "You little ...!" Then he uses a word which I don't think is proper English. In a second he's back up on his feet and he throws himself at me.

When the lift doors open on the ground floor we're locked together, like two boxers in a ring. The people who are waiting for the lift try to pull us apart. They're used to Sam and me fighting. They see the same thing almost every day.

"That wee Omar's a trouble-maker!" someone says.

"That Sam shouldn't be picking on the poor wee boy!" says someone else who's on my side.

Sam pushes me away from him. "He hit me first!"

I jump to my feet. "He's right! He's not lying. I did hit him first. I admit it. I won't be anybody's poor wee boy."

"You don't use words right!" Sam shouts at me.

"I can speak two languages!" I tell him. "You still have trouble with English."

Sam doesn't like me saying this at all. He grabs at me and yells at the top of his voice, "I'm going to get you for that!"

I jump up and down. "Get me! Get me!" Then I decide to run. Sam is bigger than me. And I think he can run faster.

He chases me all the way to school. Mrs Hart, our teacher, roars at Sam because he's given me a black eye.

"Look at his nose," I tell her, and I point at the blood still trickling from his nostrils. "I did that!"

She doesn't listen. "What does that say?" she says and points to the poster on the wall. The poster's there to teach all of us in the class about tolerance. This is a very hard word for me to learn, but it's a very important word to know. It means understanding and respecting everyone even if they're different from you. The poster also tells us how we must treat the asylum seekers who have moved into the area with respect. It says we must all live together in peace.

Sam peers at it, then he turns away in disgust. "I don't like him!" He points at me. "And no poster on the wall is going to make me like him."

"You're skating on thin ice, Sam!" the teacher says. I don't understand. There's no ice at all in the classroom. And Sam definitely has no skates.

Sam gets extra homework and a letter is sent home to his parents. I have to take a letter home to my family too. My father won't be very happy about this letter.

At school, Sam and his friends never leave me alone. They know that if they pick on me, I'll fight back. Then I'll get into trouble too.

They crowd round me in the school canteen. I throw a pizza at Sam. It hits him right in the face.

"No wonder they threw you out of your country!" Sam says to me. He picks pepperoni out of his hair.

My father would be very angry at such a waste of food. But I'm angry too.

"They did not throw me out! I left!" I shout.

I don't add that my family and I left in the middle of the night, hidden in the secret compartment of a truck.

"I wish they'd come and take you back! We don't want you here!" Sam yells at me.

I know what you're thinking. Why did I tell my cousin Chat that this Sam is my best friend, when everyone can see that, in fact, he hates me?

The truth is, of course, that Sam isn't my best friend. He's not a friend at all. But I can't tell my cousin Chat this. He's longing to be here with me. When he writes to me, he tells me all to me about it. He's always afraid in our own country. Soon, I hope he can join me and I don't want him to be afraid about being here as well. So when I write to him I tell him about the wonderful things that he can look forward to, and the fun he'll have with my friend, Sam.

Is this wrong of me?

Chapter 3
My Mother, the Boxer

When I get home my mother has had
words with Mrs Brown. A little more than
words. In fact they were locked in mortal
combat and the neighbours had to separate
them.

Mrs Brown had complained about the
smell of cooking coming from our house.

She told my mother the smell of spices
and herbs is bad for you. My mother told Mrs

Brown she wouldn't know a good meal if it hit her in the face. (As you can see, my mother has picked up English faster than I have.) That was when Mrs Brown hit my mother in the face.

This could have turned into World War 3. My father says we must always try to get on with our neighbours. We are guests in this country. My mother told him to shut up.

I sometimes think my mother and Mrs Brown could be really good friends if they tried. They're very alike. They have no tolerance.

When I come home with my letter from Mrs Hart, it only makes things worse.

"I will have no fighting!" my father tells me.

My mother puts an arm around me. She's on my side. "And I will not have him being picked on!" she snaps back.

I agree with my mother about this. I can't let Sam pick on me. I never want to be anyone's victim ever again.

But I remember too, that I was a lot like Sam back in my old country. I was always picking on my cousin, Chat.

****

My dear cousin Chat,

The weather here is raining. It rains a lot in this country. So, there will never be a drought when everything dries up. In our land we have droughts too often. But here it rains. In fact, it is always raining cats and dogs. I do not know why they say this. I have never seen any cats or dogs when it rains. English is a very funny language. My friend Sam has another way of saying what the weather is like, but Mrs Hart, our teacher, gave him one hundred lines when he said it. She said he was rude. But everyone else in the class laughed.

Mrs Hart says that because there is so much rain in this country, the trees here are the richest shades of green, and the grass grows lush and thick. And she is right. I have never seen such lovely colours. The rain brings many blessings.

But when you come, bring an umbrella.

I hope you will love this country as much as I do, Chat. The people are friendly, and our home is safe and warm. I wish so much you were here with me.

Do not worry about your father. He will be let out of prison soon. My father too was arrested. Remember? And soon he was free, and we could hardly see the scars and the bruises he had got.

When you come here I promise things will be different. I will not bully you or beat you, or make you feel bad. I am sorry for all that. All that is over and done. My friend Sam has taught me that bullying is not a good thing. To make someone feel always afraid is bad. I am ashamed, Chat. When you come here, I promise, I will be your friend.

Your cousin and your friend, Omar.

Chapter 4
Sam's Secret

I leave my house to go and post the letter. It's early evening. It is still raining. The rain means Sam and his friends are sitting inside our flats, on the ground floor.

They all stand as soon as they see me. They block my way. I try to stand tall, show them I'm not afraid. But inside I'm shaking.

"So where are you off to, wee Omar?" Sam asks me.

"It's none of your business," I tell him.

I know this'll only make him angry with me. Why don't I keep my mouth shut?

I try to hide my letter behind my back but Sam sees it. "Who have you got to write to?" he says. "You've not got any friends!"

"That too is none of your business," I shout. Why do I always make Sam angry like this? But he gets right up my nose. This is another saying here. I do not understand it. But I like the sound of it. He gets right up my nose.

"You're living in my country. That makes it my business." This makes no sense, but then does Sam never makes sense.

He reaches out to grab the letter from my hand. I side-step him and he trips up and falls on the ground. This only makes him more angry. "Grab him!" he yells to his friends.

Suddenly, they are after me. I run. I don't want them to catch me. I don't want them to read my letter. I race out of the flats and along the lane. Because of the rain the streets are empty and I splash through puddles as I run upstairs and downstairs. I race through back gardens, past blocks of flats, behind empty, broken down old shops. I'm going round in circles. My legs hurt. I can hardly breathe. But I can't let them catch me. At last, I turn up a dark street. But to my horror it's a dead end.

Dead end. That's a good way to tell you how I feel, when I see there's nowhere else for me to run.

They're running towards me. I can hear them coming closer. I turn to face them. I'm afraid, but I won't show it. I'll fight them if I

have to. They grab me by the arms and pin me against the wall. They're a lot bigger than me and it's no good me trying to get away.

Where are all those nosy neighbours now, I ask myself?

Keeping out of the cats and dogs, I think.

Sam swaggers up to me and plucks the letter from my hands. With a sneer he rips open the envelope and throws that to the ground. I watch as his eyes scan my letter. They look at each word, each line, each page.

I wait for him to mock me. To laugh at me. He'll laugh at me for saying how much I love this country and how friendly the people are. Most of all, he'll laugh for calling him my best friend.

How will I ever live this down? I've always tried not to have anyone, most of all Sam, laugh at me or think I'm a fool. I don't want anyone to feel sorry for me. I'd rather be picked on than have their pity.

I'm trying not to cry.

Sam looks at the letter for a long time. Then he turns his eyes on me. His voice is a snarl. "What's all this?"

He waves the letter in front of my face. I begin to stammer. I'm trying hard to think of something that will get me out of this.

He doesn't wait. He turns to his friends. "He's written it in his poxy language. I can't understand a word. It's rubbish!" And Sam stuffs the letter back in my pocket. "I swear, they should have to learn English before they come here."

I'm weak at the knees as if I'm about to faint.

Sam begins to walk away from me. "Come on, boys. He's not worth the bother."

I'm stunned into silence. I'm gobsmacked. My gob has never been so smacked.

Sam hasn't given me away. But why? He had it in his power to have them all laughing at me. To make me look a fool. But he didn't say anything.

Why?

Sam read my letter but he didn't tell his friends what I'd written!

And suddenly, the answer comes to me.

Sam's always in trouble at school for not paying attention.

Sam does badly in tests.

The other day when the teacher asked him to read the poster, he made an excuse. He always makes excuses.

And now I know why.

Sam can't read.

Chapter 5
Power

I think about what I've worked out all night and all the next day. Sam can't read. He wouldn't be able to read my letter. It wouldn't mean anything to him. He thought that I'd written to my cousin in my own language. But because he can't read, Sam didn't see that I wrote in English. All writing's the same to him.

Next day at school Sam sees me watching him.

He watches me. All the day long.

Can he see that I know his secret? I don't think so.

In the canteen I see he's looking hard at the menu. I have a plan to test him.

"What are you having to eat today, Sam?" I ask him and then I point at the line on the menu board which says Cheese Pasta. "Please can you tell me – what does that say? My English is not good."

Sam stares at me as if I'm a fool. "Oh, and I thought you were so smart!" he shouts at me. "D'you think I'm going to help you?"

Another clue. I am right.

I test him again in class. Mrs Hart is writing on the whiteboard. I pull at Sam's sleeve. "What is she writing there?"

He's looking at the whiteboard too. For a moment he forgets it's me who's asking. "I can never read her writing," he says. Then he turns on me. "What is this! Who do you think you are? Buzz off."

But now I am sure. I know the truth. Sam can't read.

"What are you looking so pleased with yourself for?" Sam asks me as I walk past him out of the school gates. I can't help but feel pleased with myself.

Sam doesn't want his friends to know he can't read.

He doesn't even want Mrs Hart to know he can't read. I could tell on him, and his friends would laugh at him. Then everyone would know. One word from me. That's all it would take and I could stop Sam from ever picking on me again.

I could say to him, "Stay back from me, or I will tell everyone you cannot read."

Now I have the power over Sam.

Chapter 6
Out of the Bag

When I go to the lift next morning, Mrs Brown is already there waiting for it too. When she sees me she aims her umbrella at me as if it was a soldier's gun. Her invisible friend is with her.

"Here he comes," Mrs Brown says to this invisible friend of hers. "Here's the boy whose mother tried to kill me to death! Look at that!" She points to a tiny mark on her cheek. "Your mother did that."

I think it's better not to say anything about my mother's black eye at that point.

"I'm very sorry," I say. I can afford to be nice to Mrs Brown. My father told me last night that we should be kind to people who are a bit simple. Mrs Brown is more that a bit simple. I shall be nice to Mrs Brown from now on.

It's Sam I want to see. Because I have made up my mind. I know what I will do. Sam will never pick on me again. If he does, I will let the cat out of the bag. Something else that people say that I don't understand. I've never seen a cat jumping out of a bag when you find out a secret. Where do these wonderful sayings come from? I love English!

Sam steps into the lift at the 10th floor. Mrs Brown says to her friend, "Here comes another one looking for trouble." She lifts her umbrella as if she wants to protect herself from Sam.

When she does that, I suddenly see that Mrs Brown's problem is not with me. She doesn't like children. Any children. I shouldn't take it personally.

Sam stares at me.

I stare at Sam.

"What are you looking at?" he snarls.

In a moment I'm going to tell him all I know. Warn him he must be nice to me. Or else, I'll tell the world his secret. I will let the cat out of the bag. But I don't speak.

I can say nothing. Suddenly, my mouth is dry as dust.

I think of my father. The soldiers warned my father to stop helping the sick or he would go to prison. Yet he risked going to prison because he wanted to do the right thing. "You must always do the right thing, Omar," he says to me. "Or else for the rest of your life you will feel bad."

I don't want to feel bad for the rest of my life.

I know in that moment, that I'll never tell anyone about Sam.

So it's Sam who says something first. And what he says makes my eyes pop from my head.

"Why did you tell your cousin I was your best friend?"

This makes me feel as if I've lost my voice. As if there's a frog in my throat. That's another saying I don't understand. But I do feel as if a family of frogs and some seahorses too are stuck in my throat.

"You told him I was your best friend," Sam goes on. "Ha! You wish!"

At last I can say something. "Can you read?"

"Of course I can read," Sam says. Then his mouth drops open and he starts shouting at me. "What do you mean, can I read? I go to the same school as you. I've been speaking English for years! Of course I can read"

I'm trying hard to work all this out.

"But ... but, you did not tell your friends what was in my letter?"

Sam doesn't answer. All he says is, "Do you really think this is a wonderful country?"

"Yes," I tell him at once. "I can go to school. I go home, I eat my dinner. I am not in any danger."

Sam grins at me. Yes. He actually smiles. "You're always in danger from me."

I shake my head. "But you would not shoot me, or my family."

He stares at me for a long time. "Would they shoot you in your country?"

I nod. "Many of my father's friends were shot. My father was arrested and tortured. Yes, Sam, this is a wonderful country. I do not ever want to leave."

I'm waiting for him to say something nasty, but he doesn't. "What made you pick me as a friend?" he asks.

"I do not know." This is a lie. When I came to this country I wanted a friend so badly, and I wanted to tell my cousin Chat that I had made one right away. I remember that first day at school. I saw Sam, laughing with his friends, playing football, making jokes. He seemed to be having so much fun and I thought how great it would be if I was playing football with him, laughing with him. I wanted to be his friend.

But I'll never tell Sam this. Sam would just laugh if I told him all that. And I don't want anyone to feel sorry for me.

I see that Sam's thinking about all this. He's thinking so hard, he's frowning. All at once his eyes open wide. "Wait a minute," he says. "You really thought I couldn't read, and you didn't tell on me?"

I say to Sam, "And you knew my letter was full of rubbish, but you didn't tell your friends about me."

Sam stares at me for a moment. Then he grins. "So we didn't tell on each other. That's pretty cool when you think of it."

Mrs Brown has been watching all this with interest. She turns up her hearing aid. "What are you two boys whispering about? You're up to something, I can see that!" Suddenly, she lifts her umbrella and begins to hit us both with it.

The lift doors open. People have heard the yells. They are waiting, ready to separate Sam and me again. And what do they find?

Two boys being beaten to death by an elderly woman with her umbrella.

They all begin to laugh.

"Someone save us!" Sam shouts. But he's laughing too.

"This is against the law!" I yell, but I laugh too.

Mrs Brown has to be dragged away from us. "You're evil, both of you!" she shouts. "One's as bad as the other!"

Chapter 7
Under the Skin

I'd like to say that Sam and I are best friends now. But that wouldn't be true. I can say we're no longer enemies.

When we go down in the lift together, we never fight now. Sometimes we walk together to school, kicking a football between us. He tells me jokes I never understand. He says I laugh in all the wrong places. English is a very funny language. And when Mrs Brown chases us, we always run together and hide.

She thinks we're planning to do something terrible to her.

There are still times when we argue. But we never fight. I don't think we'll ever fight again.

In fact, I think Sam and I are a lot alike. Mrs Hart says that we are brothers under the skin. I didn't know what that meant. Nor did Sam. Mrs Hart told us. It means that even if we're different outside, we are exactly the same inside.

"I understand now," I said when she told this to us. "I'm handsome and Sam is ugly, but inside he's as good looking as I am."

Sam grabs at me. "You won't be so good looking if I give you another black eye!"

But we're laughing, and even Mrs Hart smiles.

She smiles because she knows there will be no more black eyes for Sam and me.

Sam says I've made him look again at this wonderful city we live in. He says, now he thinks this country's pretty cool. I still think it's cold and damp.

But Sam has taught me many things too.

****

My dear cousin Chat,

What wonderful news. You are coming at last. I cannot wait to see you. You will have a wonderful time in this country. I will make sure of it. Mrs Hart is a good teacher, even if she is always shouting at us. She says Sam and I are going to drive her potty. I do not understand, as Sam and I are too young to drive her anywhere. But I know that you will like Mrs Hart. You and I will go to school together and play football. We will make many friends. I have told my friend Sam you will be here soon and he says he cannot wait. He says he is going to wind you right up when you come here, as if you were a clock! I do not know what it means, but I think it sounds like fun.

Your friend, your cousin, your buddy, your mate, your pal, and soon your room mate,

Omar

Our books are tested
for children and young people by
children and young people.

Thanks to everyone who consulted on
a manuscript for their time and effort in
helping us to make our books better
for our readers.

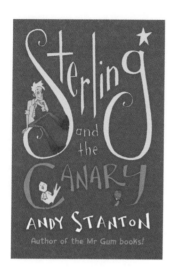

Sterling and the Canary
by
Andy Stanton

Lizzie Harris won't go out with Sterling Thaxton. Sterling needs help, but who can he ask? Not his friend Doctorr Edward Macintosh — that would be too embarrassing. Perhaps a canary would do the trick?

Hostage
by
Malorie Blackman

Blindfolded.
Alone.
Afraid.
Angela has no idea where she is. No idea what will happen next. All she knows is that she has been kidnapped.
Can she find the courage to escape?

You can order these books directly from our website at
www.barringtonstoke.co.uk